LISA LISA

Other works by the author include

A N T H O N Y   B A R N E T T

L I S A   L I S A

Two Prosays

A B ©
M M

Published by Allardyce Book
imprint of
Allardyce, Barnett, Publishers
14 Mount Street, Lewes, East Sussex BN7 1HL
e-mail: abarnett@appleonline.net

Distributed in USA by SPD Inc

website: www.spdbooks.org

Typeset by AB©omposer
in Joanna MT with title in Elisabeth BG
Printed by ARowe

A CIP record for this book is available from
The British Library and The Library of Congress

ISBN 0 907954 28 6

Contents

LISA'S STORY

I DECIDED TO TELL Lisa a story. Because of Lisa I had begun to read a novel that begins with a confusing parable about encounters between a Catholic missionary and three Aztec priests who receive the miraculous gift of being able to walk on water. Across the sea towards a ship. At least, I found it confusing, or I found confusion in it, until I came to the last pages of the novel in which I sensed an attempt to reconcile, to diffuse, that confusion. Because I did not want to find the parable so confusing. Although perhaps I still do. Also I wanted to like the novel more than I did. As I read the parable I was reminded of another parable that I thought I preferred in which a Hindu monk and a Buddhist monk arrive at a river that they wish to cross. The Hindu monk begins to walk on the water but the Buddhist monk called after him Come back. That is not the way to cross the river. Whereupon they walk a little distance along the bank of the river until they came to a place where the water, forming a ford, was shallow enough to wade through. Which might be the miracle of the depths and the shallows amid confusion in the past and the present.

POSTSCRIPT

I went on to read other novels by the same author. The first, or rather, the second that I read, his most famous, I believe, which I found almost unconditionally likeable, despite feelings of unease, contains this wonderful riddle of the sands: If a thing happens once it can never happen again. But if a thing happens twice it will always happen a third time. But what I take to be the false, at best dubious, if I try to be charitable, prophet professing morality of the second, or rather the third that I read, or rather that I am still in the process of reading, so that I cannot know exactly what I might feel by the last page, seems to me quite (distasteful would be too effete) offensive, hardly redeemed by whatever flashes of wisdom it has to offer. Yet I have also to remark the extraordinary coincidence of the proximity of its geographical setting, and the naming in its pages of a certain Road which is there to guide pilgrims to a certain City, with the Detour leading to that same City which is the title of a beautiful account of a cultural pilgrimage, by a different author of remarkable novels, that I had recommended (noting it down) on the first occasion on which Lisa and I have so far met.

On the 31st of July

THE WRITER WISHES HIS COUNTRY WERE OTHER
THAN IT IS AND DISCOVERS HOW TO FICTIONALIZE
EPISODES IN HIS LIFE FOR A MOTION PICTURE

O N THE 31ST OF JULY the poet, publisher, editor, translator and *amateur* musicologist A. Childe decided to assert his moral right, in accordance with section 77 of the Copyright, Design and Patents Act 1988, to be identified as the author of the following story, by writing it down, with the intention of issuing it for sale in a limited edition. In fact, Abi detested that usual form of the wording of part of the copyright notice to be found on the verso of the title pages of most books published in the Isles in which he felt, from a cultural point of view, he had too long, for his own good, been domiciled, from which he wished he could escape more often than he felt able, or wished were other than they were, a wording by no means mandatory. For his tiny imprint he had formulated, quite independently, a less offensive wording, similar to that used by another *larger* publisher, stating simply that *so-and-so is hereby identified as the author in question.* As a further nod in the direction of what he thought about this tautological nonsense, a type of legalese he assumed, he had added to one of his books the lines

> moral right immoral wrong
> a cert is asserted

What is certain is that at some point in the middle of that particular night, in the earliest hours of the morning, the Isle (or, correctly speaking, Isles) of which, according to his passport, he was a reluctant citizen was turned on its head, upside down, not in the sense that a room or a desk drawer is turned over during the search for a mislaid or suspected item, or trashed, or in the sense that disorder and confusion already reign, explaining why the item has been lost in the first place, but literally. Inhabitants who slept soundly did so in ignorance until they awoke the next morning, with the exception of those for whom the event, as it came to be known, was a dream come true, or for whom it had become a nightmare—as in *If I cannot live my daydreams all I am left with are my nightmares.* Lovers felt the earth move, revellers thought it par for the course, insomniacs were phased, and night-shift workers nonplussed. The peaks and the troughs of the North of the Isle were now positioned in the South. The plains and foothills of the South were now positioned in the North. The valleys and the lakes of the West in the East and the wetlands of the East

14

in the West. What was not immediately clear was whether what was not a fixture, be it animate or inanimate, had remained *in place* or whether all that had moved along, *around*, with the landscape. With good reason, as it turned out, because by midday it had become apparent that certain things had not, while other uncertain things had. Water, which usually follows its own course, threw in its lot with the latter. Bear in mind that the ways of the gods are not perfect, the devil, as it is said, being in the detail, and creational, as much as recreational, upheavals of this kind, however scientifically or imaginatively formulated (whether or not they are intended to correct yesterday's evolutionary errors) are likely to introduce new up-to-the-minute mistakes.

*

He thought this suspension of belief, which might just as well be disbelief, perfectly acceptable. He was after all writing a fiction. Off hand he knew two precedents in which authors he held in the highest regard had tampered with the geographical features of their native lands. One in which Portugal had broken off from the Spanish mainland to sail away from the Iberian Peninsular. Another in which the Netherlands had assumed a southernmost mountainous aspect, somewhat Spanish in character. Miraculous regions for whatever reasons. Abi wanted to imagine a

Britain in which he felt more at home and this is the way it seemed to him to be possible. Yet he was getting bogged down from tireless, tiresome efforts at reconciling what was probably irreconcilable. He wondered whether he would ever be able to finish, or even continue, his story satisfactorily. What happens next? he asked himself.

*

Lack of staying power. I've often lacked staying power, he said. It's a block of some kind. I call it a bloc, without the k. That's how it's spelt in French. Xavier looked at him across the table. K for Kant, he said. No, c for can't. *Can't and the Platypus. Pussy and the Platypus.* Or cant. They paused. Why not c for cantor? That'll do. Or b for banter. Let's drink up and we can look at the location. Abi tilted his head back to drain his serré. There's a c and a k in Kalck, he said, two ks in fact. And an h in Bloch, said Xavier. His books were mathematical structures, which isn't my idea. I don't think it takes account of . . . *in-expectation.*

*

Tell me about London. Abi was silent for a moment. Longer than a moment. What happened? What happens in this scene? The anti-hero, we'll call him A, for anti-. And we'll call her M. The last letter of the first half of the alphabet. I am. a.m. A tries to see M. At the Slade. Before she enrolled in the Film School. No. After. I'm not sure. It's tragic. It has the elements of a tragedy but in the long run it probably isn't that. Just a cliché. A fraught chase through the busy streets. They jump on and off a bus. He hammers down a door. It's late afternoon, early evening, by now. She lets him in, she doesn't really have an alternative, she cannot easily avoid him, she has to face him stoically. Probably she is no longer afraid, not physically, but resigned. Psychologically I'm not sure. Impassive. She lets him talk, lets him stay the night. He's in a bad state of mind, affecting the functioning of his body. He can't do a thing. *The Platypus.* Two years of intense unconsummated intimacy. Beautiful games. Once only she has untruly *he was led to think* offered herself, at an impossible moment. She returns unannounced–he doesn't know–from a vacation in America, precipitating his break-down, heralded by five days and nights of uncontrollable weeping, from which he has notionally recovered. Now, at this moment, their fates intervene, he's impotent. She's rigid but he is not. Does this mean they both avoid greater certain humiliation? She's lying there, unmoving. Prepared. An anagram. Pretending? The only way she knows. It doesn't work. How could it? Does she know? She's still a virgin. Yes and no. She says Yes. She knows No. Responsibility. Guilt. Pity. Chastisement. Desire. Which is it? Later, much later, he is secretly in awe, relieved, almost thankful that she handles this herself, with no outside interference. He feels bound to her by failure. Either she believes he is harmless enough or that his love, painfully unreciprocated . . . words fail him. Or that she deserves what she gets. Something or nothing. This happens in England's Lane. M is a Washington-born I– I'd better not say. M is for Moslem. Muslim. A is supposed to be Jewish. A for Arab. I've checked up. It has an apology. I mean apostrophe. Not all street names do. Nothing to write home about. Funny? No.

*

Why try to write in the manner of writers he admires and get hung up about not being able to do it? What is it he admires in them? Their *inimitable* voices.

*

The twice daily exchanges in cafés with Xavier Kalck, the son of his close friends, psychiatrist and radiologist, in Paris, on the point of directing his first feature, provide Abi with the opportunity to recall incidents in the past he would prefer to forget with the object of fictionalizing or prosaying them. Some will make their way into the final script, others will be too fragmentary or distracting. He has spoken about this paradox before but he wishes to express it again in another way which makes little or no sense, because he knows it is not true: A writer needs his memories like a hole in the head. Abi himself will make an appearance in the film. Xavier has already shot what amounts to a screen-test.

*

In the screen-test Xavier sits on a bench, smoking. Abi approaches off-screen picking up manuscript pages scattered on the embankment. He sits down and begins scribbling with a pencil given him by Xavier, whom he appears not to know. Abi gathers up his papers and takes off. Some other business with a shoulder holdall and an old movie camera.

*

It's very strange, Abi says. While I was translating those poems of Zanzotto's . . . What is it with these letters? Look at his initials, A. Z., Andrea Zanzotto . . . I came across his poem "Lanternina cieca", from Pasque, in which Neta and Toni figure. Now, these are diminuitives, is that the right word, of Annette and Anthony. Pet names. [cf. Z's petél.] These are the characters in the story that's set in Oslo. But important scenes also take place on the steps of the Greek theatre at Taormina, and in the bedroom of the hotel with the orange tree or the lemon tree in the garden, or is it a courtyard, during the Easter vacation. *Pasque.* One day they hired a car, drove up half-circling Etna which he is amazed to discover is an anagram of Neta, where they are harassed by a group of youngsters in a little Fiat on the way down. Another day they drove along the coast, past the villa in *The Godfather*, only to be harassed by a man who seeks them out on a deserted beach, populated by pines. He advises them to leave. It might be dangerous, he says, to park there and picnic. Not before he has touched her on her thigh. With her jet black hair she might be taken for a Mediterranean, though her skin has a rosemaling flush and she has that marble Nordic stance.

*

For years the coastal resort of Taormina has hosted a poetry prize. Xavier wonders whether their budget is going to be sufficient to get the whole company to Oslo as well as Taormina. A skeleton crew might suffice. Two actors, cameraman, director, the rest locals.

*

Nette, who is Annette, has in the past called him a sucker for reason. In the room in Taormina she flings accusatively back at him a line from one of his poems: You say in one of your poems that you're a tyrant and a martyr. This vies for the occasion on which she spat at him. He stops short. This has no answer. Yes, meekly he agrees that he wrote the line: I am tryant and martyr. It comes from a poem in his book *Fear and Misadventure*. Auto-allusion to Kierkegaard? Misadventure is a lexical concept practically unknown in Norwegian. He believes it falls between a mistake and a misunderstanding. Dano-Norwegian legal terminology has to settle for an accident or negligence. His Norwegian translator found a solid solution. *Bange anelser*. Apprehensions. Misgivings. Years later he sees that she has trumped him. Innocently but advantageously. He never said what she accused him of saying. The previous line reads: In front of no one. So the meaning is quite different, opposite almost. He has allowed himself to be misquoted, has acquiesced in her big little misunderstanding, with the most disastrous consequences. Or would things have turned out the way they did anyway, since things had already come to a pretty pass. What if he had had the presence of mind to say, No, that is not what the poem says? And, anyway, did I ever say that the persona in the poem is the poet? Just who do you think you are kidding, he can picture her thinking. A rhetorical question in no need of a question mark.

*

Lisa and I arranged to meet at three the following afternoon at the café just across the bridge on the Île St-Louis.
The name escapes me but you can't miss it. I had a lunch
appointment with Yola at twelve in the garden of the
Musée Rodin which would give us enough time to discuss
progress on the texts to be published with her paintings,
and for me to walk over to the Île afterwards. Yola arrived at
twelve-thirty. We chatted while we shared an average salad.
I have never liked queuing, preferring to be seated and
waited upon when it comes to restaurants.

*

Abi suddenly felt the onset of the recurrent failure of nerve
and doubts that periodically beset him. Why torment himself? Once again he had begun to think back to a fateful
night, one of several, he reminded himself, as a distraction
from the events of the thirty-first of July–no, of course, that
was the day he began to write down the story, nowhere did
he say that that was the night of the event–as well as an unre-
solved correspondence about a dispute over revisions to
a co-authored entry in a dictionary of music. The editor
and the co-author, infantine and journeyman, heard exactly
what he heard but, siding together to oppose him, inter-
preted differently what was significant and what was not
significant in the field of improvisation. Abi was neither

an accomplished musician—string instruments possessing more than one string not being among those he could play at all—although, brimming with brilliant ideas, he had, with freely acknowledged good fortune, perfect timing, determination and fortitude, performed occasionally with sympathetic professionals, nor, as the others were, was he capable of transcribing a solo or following music notation quickly. Thus self-confidence in his violinistic and musical opinion could not be bolstered by recourse to any technical or academic credential. In the course of correspondence with the virtuoso violinist/now conductor P. Z., residing in New York, Abi had formulated a Shakespearean defence of the position in which he might find himself on being confronted by anyone who would ask how, despite the critical acclaim that greeted publication of his half-a-life-time's research, he could possibly consider himself an authority on such a subject, that, until now, but for him, he supposed, had remained largely arcane: Has not a Jew ears? To which said v/n c had replied: As long as the ears have not been circumcised.

*

Abi wondered whether he should move the setting of the alteration to the geography of the Isles to the eleventh of August, the day of the forthcoming eclipse. A nice idea, and time enough, but hardly practical because the eclipse would begin and end in broad daylight, however misted or clouded over. As the story currently unfolded he foresaw difficulty establishing whether or not eclipse pilgrims were making for the wrong sites. On further reflection, perhaps not, because this was only the Isles turned upside-down, not the World.

*

I asked Yola the time because it was there on her wrist, not in a pocket as mine was. We looked at her watch. Quarter past. Shall we leave? In five minutes or so. We walked out of the gardens close to half past. I was beginning to worry that I would not get to l'Île St-Louis on time, that Lisa, not finding me where I said I would be, at a café, salon de thé, de glace, that she did not know, would not wait, assuming that I had never intended to meet her a second time in the first place, that I would never know whether or not she herself, perhaps, understandably having had second thoughts, had kept our rendezvous. Yola, who was not pressed for time, wanted to show me the quickest way. Much to her amusement, my sense of direction in unfamiliar streets conspired with my increasing anxiety in telling me that we must be going in the wrong direction, or at least taking the wrong shortcuts, which we were not. The hour was fast approaching. Notre Dame in sight, the river not yet crossed. We arrived at Pont St-Louis five minutes past. Yola reassured me that, according to etiquette [in deference to the forest's galateo], I was not late, and went her way. I reasoned that if Lisa had already arrived she was certainly not going to disappear after five minutes. I scanned the crowded tables outside in the bright light, poked my head round the door where there were just a few people, came out again and sat down at the only easily available vacant table. I had played a waiting game before, though I had never thought it a game, with very painful results. For M in the rain, for example. By quarter past I was scribbling nonsense in my notebook, trying to look like a writer, as if to keep occupied, twenty past I decided I was no longer waiting for anyone, simply enjoying a tisane in the sun, between half past and a quarter to, astonishment. My watch said nearly a quarter to. A quarter to what? Three. I had sat down just after two, thinking it was three. Yola! I hurried you across Paris when we had another whole hour to spare. Now I'm red in the face. I felt a wave of relief, embarrassment, and naïve restored faith in Lisa, the world and myself. I picked up the little tray with the pot and the cup and the saucer, and motioned to the waiter to let him know I had decided on the cool of the interior. I chose a table along the back wall with a panoramic view of the several large windows, a bit like a series of photos placed in a spread, and began to write something that made sense.

*

Lisa appeared not one minute late striding past the tables in her long sarong-like skirt. I jumped up to call out to her from the entrance. She saw me and came in and we greeted each other affectionately. Yesterday we had parted with a handshake. Today she wore a white T-shirt, in place of the slip, covering her discreet shoulder tattoo, transfer or permanent I knew not. It's like Vienna, she said, looking around at the décor. I thought you would like it. If you order coffee it comes with delicious chocolates. No, just an orange juice.

*

We had no wish to queue to see Manet's nymphs and eventually ended up in another café with a carafe of rosé, brought by a waiter with handlebar moustache who mockingly tut-tutted and shook his head when I ordered a carafe of water and no absinthe alongside, which loosened tongues and in due course I told Lisa she was beautiful, to which her reply was properly modest. I have reason too to be grateful to Lisa for her consideration in the light of the mistake I felt I had made in suggesting what turned out to be a futile trek to get to see the nymphs. Je suis desolé, I said, turning to her at one point while we were making our way back along a crowded sidewalk, looking for a pleasant corner café bar such as the one in which we now found ourselves. But I soon concluded that she did not direct any disappointment she may have felt at her companion of the moment or that she thought any the less of him. She was not a woman with whom one was obliged to tread on eggshells.

*

I had complimented her the day before. Lisa's English, spoken in the Scottish accent she had acquired in Edinburgh was perfect. Nothing in her voice indicated that she was not British and she had made no mistakes until now. I thought that if she were a spy, an Austro-Hungarian spy, nothing gave her away. All of a sudden she did. Lisa you've made your first mistake in English. One that is common enough among Scandinavians, German speakers too, I imagine, it must be something to do with the syntax. You said: I don't hope so. Instead of: I hope not. I wondered what I'd said. I saw your eyes alight somewhere, Lisa said.

*

Lisa, I said, planting a kiss on her lips. Is this the beginning or the end of a beautiful friendship? At the time it did not seem like a cliché but an appropriately spontaneous way to part, demanding nothing *as I thought* but her visibly confused pleasure.

*

Later that evening I telephoned to apologize to Yola, who burst into laughter, about the lost hour. Or should it be regained? I know, Yola said, I have blisters on my feet.

*

Someone is missing, said Xavier. Yes, that would be Anna, Abi said. That takes place in Copenhagen. At the end she leaves the writer and takes up with a librarian. Like the woman who left Chagall for a photographer. She tells a colleague with whom A played percussion in the ensemble Cadentia Nova Danica that he was too difficult.

*

M was studying to be a film maker. Years later her name came up in the editing credits to a documentary about the *plight* of Palestinian women in Israel that I saw late one evening on the television. After what had occurred between them it took a very long time before he could enter a cinema again without feeling sick in the pit of his stomach, to say nothing of his head. He developed an aversion to film from which I don't believe he ever fully recovered, his attitude was never the same again, as if he would no longer take the medium seriously, *were he meant to*, which doesn't mean that he doesn't sometimes enjoy it, or see the point of it, or wish that he had some small part in it, as I do now. One image stands out in particular: M's eye at the viewfinder, squinting, screwed up, imperfectly perfect. I saw almost the same thing when Nette photographed her tapestry depicting our wishful poem in *Mud Settles*. Yes, I am certain that Nette knew the work, in her fearful heart of hearts. In other words, that stance is not at all unique. But certain women take on an exceptionally seductive, attractive, becoming, professional, demeanour with it.

*

A passage from *The Man Without Qualities* strikes a chord. He leaves out the addressee's response and the ensuing argument so that the resolution of the protagonist's proposition is not disclosed.

> "What is it you do, then? I'll tell you: You leave out whatever doesn't suit you. As the author himself has done before you. Just as you leave things out of your dreams or fantasies. By leaving things out, we bring beauty and excitement into the world. We evidently handle our reality by effecting some sort of compromise with it, an in-between state where the emotions prevent each other from reaching their fullest intensity, graying the colors somewhat. Children who haven't yet reached that point of control are both happier and unhappier than adults who have. And yes, stupid people also leave things out, which

is why ignorance is bliss. So I propose, to begin with, that we try to love each other as if we were characters in a novel who have met in the pages of a book. Let's in any case leave off all the fatty tissue that plumps up reality."

I wanted to ask, Xavier said, What made you choose the name Childe? Because in Dano-Norwegian child is *barn*, like *bairn* in Scots, and the postpositive *et*, where the *t* is silent, is the definite article. Placed first *et* is indefinite. And then I was not a bar mitzvah boy which is the rite of passage into adulthood. Three strikes and I'm out. Rabbi Childe. Huh. You too. Abbé Childe. *Now that Martine, François, Myriam and Xavier grow apples atop the interred ruins of O l'Abbaye.*

*

And Lisa? Oh Lisa. I've really no idea. I don't think it was a butterfly alight on her shoulder. *Skies are . . . as "Liza Liza" goes.*

*

ON THE 11TH AUGUST 1999 Abi Childe decided to finish his story between shoots by returning to his house a few miles inland from the south coast. All that he had wanted to say but had left unsaid would have to wait for other occasions, to become other stories or to be inserted at a later date in the one he was writing now. He drove to Dieppe to board the ferry sailing at eleven forty-five in the morning. The weather was changeably cloudy and sunny, hazy or misty. As it grew dark a cold chill breezed across the water. At eleven minutes after eleven nine thirty-five British Summer Time, the time the event began at what was then the extreme south-westernmost tip of the Isles, the passengers experienced eclipse totality in the middle of the English Channel. When the sun reappeared, and the warmth returned with it, no more than a couple of minutes or so later, Abi rubbed his eyes in disbelief. Before the approach of the ferry lay a group of islands to be negotiated and, beyond them, the mountains.

BREAKING THE SPELL

That novel you spoke about, Xavier said, wasn't it the Iberian Peninsular as a whole that broke off from France and the rest of Europe, not just Portugal from Spain? And didn't you mean Broch when you said Bloch? Unless you meant Blok, which I don't think you did? And Kalck loses a k in chalk, Abi said. It's all a fiction, you don't think that thing about The Stone Raft really happened, do you? I don't know. Hang on! Why on earth not? It's happened before.

The creation of stone rafts. Land masses breaking away, moving off, becoming islands or attaching themselves somewhere else, in another place altogether. Except for the fault in the rock, of course, that stayed where it was. But is it wise for the reader to break the spell? As Hrabal put it it's all right as long as you take it with a pinch of salt. Sea or rock . . . Look at that iceberg, for example.

*

I was going to call that last—now penultimate—passage CORRI-GENDA until I found out, by a quirk of coincidence, that intelligent readers would think I had copied the word from Hrabal who has his own CORRIGENDUM in which he says: To me this fiction is all the dearer, for being less truthful, and hence more beautiful.

*

Can I stop now . . .

Yes. No. Wait. This is funny. Lisaa. Acronym for L'Institut Supérieur des Arts Appliqués. Yola has taught there and Myriam has studied there. In this story all roads lead to Lisa. That day we met I'd just bought a book about Bernhard.

Reference is made to the following works

in "Lisa's Story"
Three pseudomystic fables by Paulo Coelho
Cees Nooteboom *Roads to Santiago* [*The Detour to Santiago*]

in "On the 31st of July"
PROSE
Works in general by Thomas Bernhard
Works in general by Hermann Broch
Umberto Eco *Kant and the Platypus*
Bohumil Hrabal *Total Fears*
Robert Musil *The Man Without Qualities*
Cees Nooteboom *In The Dutch Mountains*
José Saramago *The Stone Raft*

POETRY
Andrea Zanzotto *Il Galateo in Bosco*
"Elegy in Googoo" [«L'elegia in petèl»] from *La Beltà*
"Little Dark Lantern" [«Lanternina cieca»] from *Pasque*
in *Poems by Andrea Zanzotto*, trans. A. B. Childe
A. B. Childe *Anti-Beauty*
"In green and blue . . ." from *Fear and Misadventure*
"I wish you would/warm to it, . . ." from *Mud Settles*

SONG
Gus Kahn, Ira Gershwin (words), George Gershwin (music)
"Liza (All the Clouds'll Roll Away)" from *Show Girl*

END PIECE
Journées Portes Ouvertes, Lisaa, février 2000